First Facts®

Your Favorite Authors

Nikki Grimes

by Lisa M. Bolt Simons

CAPSTONE PRESS
a capstone imprint

First Facts are published by Capstone Press,
1710 Roe Crest Drive, North Mankato, Minnesota 56003
www.mycapstone.com

Library of Congress Cataloging-in-Publication Data
Names: Simons, Lisa M. B., 1969– author.
Title: Nikki Grimes / by Lisa M. Bolt Simons.
Description: North Mankato, Minnesota : Capstone Press, [2017] | Series:
First Facts. Your Favorite Authors | Includes bibliographical references and index.
Identifiers: LCCN 2016023240| ISBN 9781515735595 (library binding) |
ISBN 9781515735649 (pbk.) | ISBN 9781515735687 (ebook (pdf))
Subjects: LCSH: Grimes, Nikki—Juvenile literature. | Poets, American—20th
century—Biography—Juvenile literature. | African American women poets—
Biography—Juvenile literature.
Classification: LCC PS3557.R489982 Z86 2017 | DDC 811/.54 [B] —dc23
LC record available at https://lccn.loc.gov/2016023240

Editorial Credits
Carrie Braulick Sheely and Michelle Hasselius, editors; Kayla Dohmen, designer;
Ruth Smith, media researcher; Gene Bentdahl, production specialist

Photo Credits
Alamy Images: WENN UK, 21, ZUMA Press, Inc., 19 L; Capstone Press: Michael Byers, cover, 17; Getty Images: Michael Ochs Archives, 13, Peter Turnley/Corbis/VCG, 9; Newscom: Handout/MCT, 19; Shutterstock: Angie Makes, cover, background design elements, arigato, cover, background design elements, DavidPinoPhotography, 5, jeafish Ping, 15 R, mandritoiu, 7, Mega Pixel, 11 T, Sean Pavone, 11 B, Sokolova23, 15 L

Printed in the United States of America.
092016   010030S17

Table of Contents

Chapter 1: First Public Reading

Nikki Grimes was nervous. The 13-year-old was giving her first poetry reading. She was at the Countee Cullen Library. It was a block away from where she was born. Grimes' dad had signed her up. He told her to look at him when she read. He thought this would calm her. The reading was the first of many public events for the future award-winning writer.

Chapter 2: Tough Childhood

Grimes was born in New York City on October 20, 1950. She started writing when she was 6 years old. She also spent a lot of time reading at libraries.

Her mom and dad separated and got back together often. Grimes and her sister spent time in **foster homes**. They had tough childhoods.

---

foster home—a place where children can live for a short time; social workers find foster homes for some children

New York City, New York

"Reading and writing were my survival tools when I was growing up. Whatever was burning in me, I took it to the page and that was my salvation." —Nikki Grimes

salvation—the saving of a person

Grimes won her first award for writing after she **graduated** from junior high school. When Grimes was in high school, her dad died. This was a tough time for her. Grimes' English teacher, Mrs. Wexler, helped Grimes focus on the future. Mrs. Wexler survived the **Holocaust**. During her junior year, Grimes met Writer James Baldwin. He became her writing **mentor**.

---

graduate—to finish a course of study in school and receive a diploma

Holocaust—the mass murder of millions of Jews, gypsies, the disabled, homosexuals, and political and religious leaders during World War II (1939–1945)

mentor—a wise and faithful adviser or teacher

James Baldwin

"[James] Baldwin was the single most important influence in my literary life. Most of all, he encouraged me to master the tools of my craft, to expand my knowledge of language, to enhance my fluency in my mother tongue."—Nikki Grimes

After high school Grimes took writing classes. She went to Livingston College of Rutgers University. Grimes earned a degree in English in 1974. She also studied African languages. Grimes won a **grant** to continue her studies. She spent a year in Tanzania in Africa.

---

grant—a gift of money given for a particular purpose

Other Interests

Grimes also lived in Sweden for six years. She hosted two radio programs. One was for **immigrants**. The other was for Swedish Educational Radio.

Stockholm, Sweden

immigrant—someone who comes from one country to live permanently in another country

Chapter 3: Where Words and Music Meet

Soon Grimes was writing her own books. She published her first book in 1977. The novel *Growin'* is about a girl who makes a new friend after her dad dies. Her first poetry book came out in 1978. Then she wrote a biography about **Activist** Malcolm X. Though poetry is Grimes' favorite, she enjoys writing a variety of books.

---

activist—a person who works to change the way things are

Malcolm X in 1965

Grimes published 12 books from 1992 to 1999. Most of these were poetry or **verse** for young people. Grimes believes children should be introduced to poetry in a positive way. She thinks poetry has magic to it. Images or last lines can be surprises. Grimes says poetry is "the place where words and music meet."

---

verse—longer poetry instead of prose

A Talented Artist

Grimes is an artist in other ways too. She once sang on stage in Sweden. She's a photographer. She also makes jewelry and other art out of paper, fabric, and fiber.

Grimes received two Coretta Scott King Book Awards in 2003. *Bronx Masquerade* won the Author Award. *Talkin' About Bessie* won an Author Honor. Three years later, Grimes earned the NCTE Award for Excellence in Poetry for Children. That same year she received a Coretta Scott King Author Honor for *Dark Sons*. The novel *Words with Wings* earned Grimes another Coretta Scott King Author Honor in 2014.

"I've tried to create books for those children who, like me, are in dark places in their childhood through no fault of their own, and who need to have that acknowledged."
—Nikki Grimes

Grimes writes about **themes** that mean something to everyone. These include friendships and family. She has shared her love of writing around the world. She has given talks in international schools.

In 2016 Grimes won the Virginia Hamilton Literary Award. This award honors authors who publish **multicultural** books.

---

theme—the main idea a written work addresses

multicultural—involving people from different races or religions

Grimes won the NAACP Image Award in 2009 for her book, *Barack Obama: Son of Promise, Child of Hope.*

BARACK OBAMA

Son of Promise, Child of Hope

NIKKI GRIMES · ILLUSTRATED BY BRYAN COLLIER

Chapter 4: Finding Her Place

Grimes has written books for all ages. She has published poetry, historical fiction, and biographies. Many of her books feature African-American characters. They deal with experiences she had as a child. She still gives poetry readings, just like she did as a nervous teenager. Grimes came out of a troubled childhood to become an award-winning writer.

Grimes in Los Angeles, California

Timeline

1950	born in New York City, New York
1956	starts writing
1963	has her first public reading
1974	graduates from Livingston College of Rutgers University
1977	publishes her first novel called *Growin'*
1978	publishes her first poetry book, *Something on My Mind*
1993	finalist for the NAACP Image Award for *Malcolm X: A Force for Change*
1999	wins her first Coretta Scott King Author Honor Award for *Jazmin's Notebook*
2003	wins the Coretta Scott King Author Award for *Bronx Masquerade*, as well as an Author Honor Award for *Talkin' About Bessie*
2006	wins the National Council of Teachers of English Award for Excellence in Poetry for Children; awarded a Coretta Scott King Honor for *Dark Sons*
2007	receives a Coretta Scott King Honor for *The Road to Paris*
2014	receives a Coretta Scott King Honor for *Words with Wings*
2016	wins the Virginia Hamilton Literary Award

Glossary

activist (AK-tuh-vist)—a person who works to change the way things are

foster home (FAWS-tuhr HOHM)—a safe place where children can live for a short time; social workers find foster homes for some children

graduate (GRAJ-oo-ate)—to finish a course of study in school and receive a diploma

grant (GRANT)—a gift of money given for a particular purpose

Holocaust (HAH-luh-cawst)—the mass murder of millions of Jews, gypsies, the disabled, homosexuals, and political and religious leaders during World War II (1939–1945)

immigrant (IM-uh-gruhnt)—someone who comes from one country to live permanently in another country

mentor (MEN-tur)—a wise and faithful adviser or teacher

multicultural (muhl-tye-KUHL-chuh-ruhl)—involving people from different races or religions

salvation (sal-VAY-shuhn)—the saving of a person

theme (THEEM)—the main idea a written work addresses

verse (VURSS)—longer poetry instead of prose

Read More

Manushkin, Fran. *It Doesn't Need to Rhyme, Katie: Writing a Poem with Katie Woo.* Katie Woo, Star Writer. North Mankato, Minn.: Picture Window Books, 2014.

Pearson, Yvonne. *Prose Poems.* Poetry Party. Mankato, Minn.: Childs World, 2015.

Wheeler, Jill. C. *Nikki Grimes.* Children's Authors. Edina, Minn.: ABDO Pub., 2011.

Internet Sites

FactHound offers a safe, fun way to find Internet sites related to this book. All of the sites on FactHound have been researched by our staff.

Here's all you do:

Visit *www.facthound.com*

Type in this code: 9781515735595

Check out projects, games and lots more at **www.capstonekids.com**